Copyright © 2000 by Lemniscaat b.v. Rotterdam
English translation copyright © 2001 by Front Street Books, Inc.
Originally published in the Netherlands under the title
Samen kunnen we alles by Lemniscaat b.v. Rotterdam
All rights reserved
Printed and bound in Belgium

CIP data is available

First U.S. edition

Beaver's Lodge

Ingrid and Dieter Schubert

Front Street 8 Lemniscaat
Asheville, North Carolina
2001

Beaver worked all day building his new lodge. He was very pleased with his work until he saw some holes in the roof.

"Oh, no, I'll have to fix those," he said.

Sighing, he climbed the lodge once again. But, then …

... he tripped. Down he fell. Thud! Beaver landed flat on his back and lay there, moaning. Fortunately Hedgehog saw everything. He ran to Beaver, shouting, "Bear, come quickly. We need your help."

Bear came running. He and Hedgehog examined
Beaver's injuries.

Beaver started crying, but not about his cuts and
scratches.

"Where will I go now?" Beaver sobbed. "My lodge is
destroyed."

Bear thought for a moment and said, "To my house."

"Great idea," said Hedgehog.
Beaver's friends carried him off to Bear's house.

Bear and Hedgehog made Beaver comfortable and
he fell asleep immediately. "Poor guy," Bear whispered.
Hedgehog agreed. Quietly they looked at their sleeping
friend.

"Shall we surprise him?" Hedgehog said suddenly.

"How?" asked Bear.

"Let's fix his lodge."

"Do you think we can?"

Hedgehog laughed. "Together we can do anything."

They walked to the lodge, which was nothing more
than a pile of rubble. Hedgehog sat down to think.
Meanwhile Bear started sorting out all the stones and
branches.

"We can't just build a new lodge. First I'll make a floor plan," Hedgehog said.

"That's smart," said Bear. "I'd never think of that."

Hedgehog drew a big cross. "We'll start here," he said.

Bear carried some sticks and stones over to the place that Hedgehog had marked. Then Hedgehog showed him how to put branches together and fill the holes with grass. Bear learned quickly.

When the lodge was high enough, Bear wanted to sit
down and take a rest, but Hedgehog said, "Can't stop
now. You still have to put mud on."

Bear gathered mud and rubbed it in all the cracks.
Hedgehog walked around the lodge and inspected it.He
pulled at the branches. Everything was very solid, but
Hedgehog shook his head slowly.

"Something is missing," Hedgehog murmured. "I just don't know what."

"Don't you think it's beautiful?" Bear asked.

Hedgehog jumped to his feet. "That's it. Let's make it the most beautiful lodge ever."

They collected a lot of decorations.

Bear and Hedgehog worked very hard. Finally the
lodge was ready. It was strong, nothing wobbled, and
it was beautiful. Bear was tired but very pleased.

"We are the best builders in the world," said Hedgehog.
They walked back to Bear's hole and woke Beaver up.

"Come on," Hedgehog said. "We have a surprise for
you."

"Don't look until we say so," said Bear.

Beaver stumbled to the lake, guided by Bear and Hedgehog. Suddenly they came to a halt.

"Now!" Bear and Hedgehog shouted.

Beaver opened his eyes wide. After a while he squeaked, "What is it?"

"Your new house, of course."

"Oh! Right ... Wow! ... Well ... Um." Beaver
paused. Then he said, "Where is the door?"

Hedgehog slapped his head. "Oh no! I knew we
forgot something!"

Bear's shoulders drooped. "Do we have to start
all over again?"

Beaver grinned and showed his teeth. "Don't
worry. I'll bite my way in."

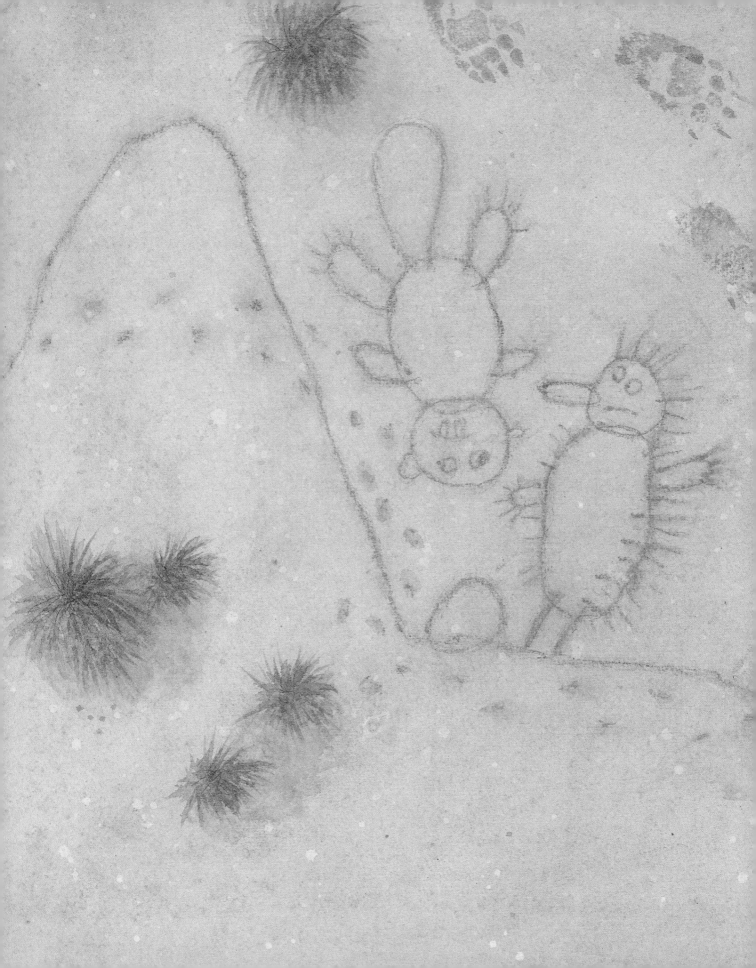